ISBN 1 85854 767 9
Published by Brimax Books Ltd, Newmarket,
England, CB8 7AU, 1998.
Printed in Spain.

THE Funny Farm

by Gill Davies   Illustrated by Gill Guile

BRIMAX

The Funny Farm

No animal is ordinary,
Each has its special charm,
But the sweetest and the funniest
Are the creatures on the Funny Farm.

There's a duck who will keep splashing
And a shorn and shivering sheep,
A donkey who plays the drums
And an owl who is trying to sleep;
One piglet is stuck in a bucket
As fox creeps up under the cart;
Cow hiccups while mice get the giggles
And frog sings of his broken heart.

Now all the animals on the Funny Farm
Are waiting to say, "Hello!"
So we hope you enjoy your visit.
It's a wonderful place to go.

Clara the Cow

Clara the cow who had hiccups
Didn't know what she should do.
"These hiccups won't leave me alone!"
She said with a HIC and a MOO.

The other cows patted her back,
And lickled her spine with a key,
And gave her a shock by BOO MOO-ing!
And leaping from out of a tree.

The farmer gave Clara some water.
"Now quickly! Gulp this all down."
She swallowed and gurgled then HICCUPed
And sighed with a sad, wrinkled frown.

"I can hold my breath counting backwards,
And roll with my feet in the air.
But these hiccups will not go away.
I really don't think it is fair."

But the hiccups were bored with HIC-MOOING
And wanted a change, so they said,
"We are leaving to drop in on Donkey
To HICCUP and HEEHAW instead!"

Penelope the Piglet

Penelope the piglet
Is very, very pink,
And very, very round
And her eyes blink wink.

Penelope the piglet
Has a squiggly, wriggly tail,
And a snuffly, wuffly snout
That is poking in a pail.

Penelope the piglet
Wants to eat up every drop.
She pushes her snout in further
And her mother shouts, "Stop!"

Now Penelope the piglet
Has her head stuck in the pail;
She roly polies in the mud
And squirms from head to tail.

She squeals and waves her trotters
Until the others pull her free;
Then says, "That pail is horrible,
It is far too small for me."

Gloria the Goose

Gloria the goose
Puts her beak up in the air,
And pretends not to notice
When the other geese stare.

She is wearing a new bonnet
With cherries on the brim,
With buttercups and braid
And a bow below her chin.

She is wearing a new dress,
With ribbons laced together
And big, frilly bloomers
And mittens made of leather.

Gloria the goose
Says, "I really do not care
What the others think
Or how very much they stare.
I like pretty things.
I feel as happy as can be."
And she dances through the fields
In her splendid finery.

Quackers the Duck

Quackers the duck likes to splash everywhere,
The others get soaked whenever he's there;
He splashes the swan, making her snort,
Then dashes away, too fast to be caught.

He splashes the drake, making him squeak,
"What is this water all over my beak?"
He splashes the goose and splashes her brother,
Then dives into the reeds to hide and take cover.

Now the swan and the geese and dripping drake,
Angry and hissing say, "Make no mistake,
Quackers the duck, you must stop being bad,
Or we'll all go away - and then you'll be sad."

Quackers says, "Sorry! I'll try to be good
And only splash where a little duck should."
But now if he feels a big splash is coming,
If his wings start to quiver, his feet start a-drumming,
He swims off alone so the others stay dry
And only comes back when the splash has passed by.

Sam Scarecrow

Sam the kindly scarecrow says,
"I am lonely as I can be.
I am meant to frighten the crows
But instead they frighten me!"

But one of the little birds
Thinks Sam is rather sweet;
So she builds her nest in his pocket,
All round and warm and neat.

She sings to Sam in the morning
He sings back, to her surprise;
And then, when her chicks hatch out,
They both sing lullabies.

Sam stands very still and quiet
When the chicks are fast asleep
But he loves to peep in his pocket
And hear them sing, "Cheep! Cheep!"

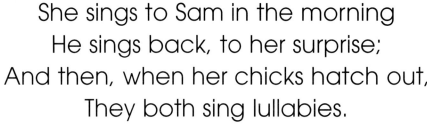

Lucy the Lamb

Lucy the lamb has lost her coat
And she doesn't know what to do.
"My wool has vanished today,
They have shorn it away."
Now she shivers and turns bright blue.

Lucy the lamb is sniffing and sneezing
And says with a sorrowful sigh,
"They have cut off my coat,
Now I look like a goat!
If I don't get it back I shall cry."

But now Lucy the lamb is happy again;
She has found something warm to wear.
She is cosy and snug,
Wrapped up in a rug,
With a woolly hat perched on her hair.

Donkey

Donkey is playing his drum set again.
He is banging and dinging,
Cymbals are ringing.
He hums and heehaws,
Then claps his applause
To his raucous and riotous singing.

The animals all run for cover again.
Piggy's eyes fill with tears
At the noise that he hears.
Mice hide in the straw,
Cats rush through the door,
And sheep pull wool right over their ears.

But Donkey thinks he makes a wonderful sound.
His big ears vibrating,
Donkey says, braying,
"It is strange when I'm playing
And singing and swaying,
How none of the others are ever around!"

Mice

Mice always seem to giggle,
Whatever you say or do;
Their tails wriggle and squiggle
And their whiskers quiver at you.

Mice always splutter and snigger
And grin with mischievous glee;
I have no idea what the joke is . . .
I just hope they're not laughing at me!

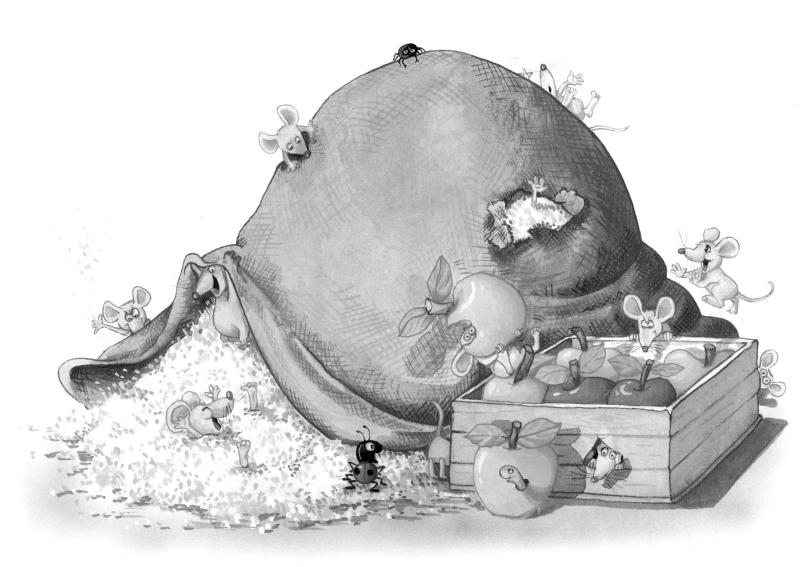

Fox

Fox is creeping through the corn
Playing hide and seek.
But the mice all run away –
"Fox is coming!" they all squeak.

Fox is creeping through the yard,
Dressed up as mother hen.
But the chickens all giggle and say,
"Here comes Fox, in disguise, again."

Fox is creeping through the barn
Silent, on tip-toes.
But the cats all laugh and cry,
"We can see your whiskered nose!"

Fox is creeping home again,
Tears streaming from his eyes.
"I only want to play," he says,
"And give them all a surprise!"

Owl

Owl tries to sleep in the old oak tree,
His head tucked under his wing.
But the daytime birds whistle and cheep,
And chatter and chirrup and sing.

Owl tries to sleep in the old farm barn,
Away from the sun's bright glare.
But the hens are having a party,
And are singing and dancing there.

Owl tries to sleep in the old farm roof,
His cap is pulled down low.
But the crows have a fight on the chimney pot
And the wind makes his feathers blow.

At last, at last, it is quiet and dark
And the sky is a midnight blue.
Owl sits up and hoots to others,
"Wake up, everybody! Twit-twoo!"

Rabbits

On the farm are some rabbits
With very bad habits
Who steal what the farmer is growing.
They come out at night
When the starlight is bright
And the pond is all silver and glowing.

They stand on their toesies
And wriggle their nosies
And listen, ears pricking, and stare.
Then off they all run
To play games and have fun
Tossing carrots and beans in the air.

Fluff the Kitten

A new, little kitten arrives at the farm.
Fluff is black with snowy white paws.
She chases the mice and the frogs and the bees
And catches wriggling string in her claws.

She peeps at the geese and the horse and the cows
But thinks, "They are too big to chase."
So she jumps in the sty and talks to the pigs,
While washing her whiskers and face.

Fluff chases the brooms as they sweep up the yard,
She chases the leaves as they blow.
Then she says to the sheep as she curls up to sleep,
"I've been terribly busy, you know!"

Spiders

The spider that hangs in the old farm barn
Is friends with the owls and the bats.
She spins pretty coats to keep them all warm,
And cradles for kittens and cats.

The spider that hangs from the stable beam
Is grumpy and cross and complaining.
He says, "It's too hot" or "Too cold" to spin webs
And, "How can I spin if it's raining?"

The spider that hangs in the hedge by the gate
Spins webs that sparkle with dew.
Then she sways in the breeze, swinging with ease
And waves at the cows passing through.

A Broken-Hearted Frog

Across the field and just beyond
Fred Frog lives in the lily pond.
He flicks his tongue and rolls his eyes
And spends the daytime catching flies.

But when the moon is high above
Fred sings about his long-lost love;
For Fred Frog loved his Nancy Newt,
He thought her speckled tum was cute.

But Nancy Newt broke poor Fred's heart
By jumping on the farmer's cart,
And riding off along the road
With smarmy, slimy Simon Toad.

So now when stars are in the skies
Fred sings, and wrings his paws, and sighs,
And stares along the farmyard track
To see if Nancy's coming back.

The Turkey Trot

Turkeys gobble, gobble, gobble,
Dancing till they're dizzy,
Stretching necks, nod-nodding heads,
Bob-bobbing, busy busy.

Turkeys dance a turkey trot,
Feet tapping on the ground,
Feathers twirling, twisting, turning,
Up and down and round.

Turkey tails whirl and swirl,
As the turkeys dance and spin,
Gobble! Gobble! Nidding, nodding,
Bobbing out and in.

Goat Hair

The goats have had their hair done:
Nanny has had a perm –
She spins to show the others
Every curly wurly turn.

Bobby has had his locks cut off,
All short and shorn and bristles;
"You are nearly bald," sing the birds,
Giggling in the thistles.

Gert is glowing, hair bright purple
And the Kid has streaks of red,
While Sue has a brilliant wig
Piled up on top of her head.

But Sally is still in her rollers
She says, "I like these best.
They are spiky and pink and pretty
And more stylish than all the rest."

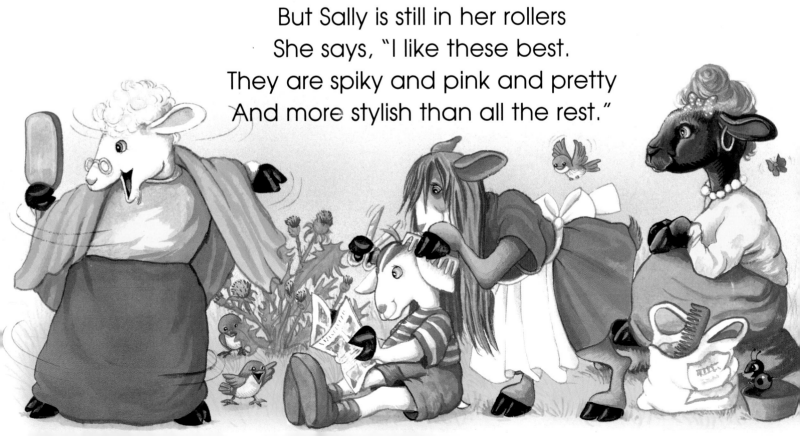

The Horse's Nightmare

The horse who has a nightmare
Dreams a funny dream one day:
His legs have shrunk too short
And he cannot reach his hay.
His ears are drooping downward,
Like the lop-eared rabbits' do;
His coat has grown all shaggy
And turned a bright, bright blue.

He peeps between his dangling ears
And says in great dismay,
"How can I run with legs like these?
And blue I cannot stay.
And when I try to talk
I bark instead of neigh.
I do not like this dream at all
Please make it go away."

Then barking, snoring, he awakes,
Legs long, and ears upright;
His nightmare's at an end
But he has had an awful fright.
"Thank heavens I am me again
What a dreadful night."
He neighs, then eats his breakfast hay,
Grinning with delight.

Hens

"It is not fair!" the hens complain,
As they bake in the midday sun,
"We should like to be in the pond
Like the ducks, who have lots of fun."

"Stop moaning," the rooster tells them,
"Just put on your swimming gear,
Go down and paddle and play –
I'll crow if the fox comes near."

So the hens put on their bathing caps
And flippers and goggles and all,
To paddle, to swim, and to snorkel
And dive where the reeds grow tall.

Sailing and racing on rafts of sticks,
They play until the sun sets,
Windsurfing and skiing, spinning around,
Getting wonderfully, blissfully wet.

Till the rooster crows out his warning,
"Quick! Hurry! The fox - he is coming!"
Then they all rush back to the yard,
Drying with towels as they're running.

Night-time

It is night-time on the Funny Farm
And the animals settle to sleep;
As the moon beams down in the yard
It is time for one last peep
At the goose in her frilly, white night-gown,
And the mice asleep in the straw,
At the donkey dreaming of drums,
And the cow with a rumbling snore.

It is night-time on the Funny Farm
And it is time to say goodbye
To the owl blinking open his eyes,
And the bats getting ready to fly.

The sheep and the pigs are smiling
As their sleepy eyes shut tight,
To rest till the rooster's call
Wakes them up in the morning light,
When another day starts on the Funny Farm.
But until then it is quiet and still
As the stars appear like clusters of jewels
At the shadowy rim of the hill.